D1371077

The Three Bears

Written by Tony Mitton

Illustrated by Tania Hurt-Newton

"Look at this door,"
said Baby Bear.
"Come on, come and see."

"Yes," said Mom and Dad.
"Just **look** at it."

"Look at this porridge,"
said Baby Bear.
"Come on, come and see."

"Yes," said Mom and Dad.

"Just **look** at it."

"Look at this chair,"
said Baby Bear.
"Come on, come and see."

"Yes," said Mom and Dad.

"Just **look** at it."

"Look at this bed,"
said Baby Bear.
"Come on, come and see."

"Yes," said Mom and Dad.
"Just **look** at it."

"Look at this **girl**,"
said Baby Bear.

"Yes," said Mom and Dad.

"Just look at her **GO**."